FANGS

By Aleesah Darlison
Illustrated by Gurihiru

Contents

Chapter 1

Ki's New Pet

"Hey, guess what Max?" Ki asked me at lunch.

Ki was my best friend. We were sitting in the school playground on our bench under the oak tree. Ki was eating a salad wrap. I was eating a ham and cheese sandwich. It tasted so **good**.

"What?" I said, with my mouth full of ham, cheese and bread.

"I got a pet on the weekend. Want to come over and see it after school?"

I looked at the ground.

A pet.

I don't like pets.

I don't like any animals at all.

Why? Because I'm afraid of them.

Mum calls it a **phobia**. Whatever it is,

I just don't like them. I know why, too.

I have kept away from all animals ever since my cousin's pet rat bit me. My finger swelled up really big. I got so sick, I had to be taken to the hospital. I was given a needle. It hurt a lot.

I didn't want that to happen again. Not ever. It was too **scary**.

I'd never told any of my friends about the rat biting me. Or about being scared of animals. Not even Ki.

Chapter 2
Ki's Pet Eats Meat

"What sort of pet?" I kept my voice steady, so Ki wouldn't know I was scared.

I thought maybe a cat or a dog. Or maybe a rabbit. I didn't like the idea of any of them.

Cats scratch.

Dogs bite.

And rabbits, well, they are soft and furry. But rabbits have **big** teeth.

Ki just zipped her lips. She grinned and said, "It's a surprise. Come to my place so I can show you."

I didn't like this at all. I needed more information. "How about a clue?"

Ki thought for a moment. "All right, then. It's **carnivorous**."

"What's that?"

"It means it only eats meat."

A shiver ran up my spine. Meat. I did not like this.

Now I imagined one of those **big**, slobbering guard dogs you see in the movies. "So, it's a dog?"

Ki shook her head. "Can't tell you."

"A really, really **mean** cat?"

"My lips are sealed."

"A bear? A lion? A hyena?"

7

Ki laughed. "I'm not telling! Are you coming over or not?"

"Maybe." Before I said yes, I needed at least one more clue. "What did you call it?"

"Fangs."

That's when I nearly choked. Fangs was not a good name. Fangs sounded **scary** and **sharp**. It did not sound cute or small. It sounded very, very dangerous.

"Does Fangs bite?"

Ki thought for a moment. "I guess you could say he does. But he hasn't bitten me yet."

"But he could, right? If you got too close, or spooked him?"

Ki laughed, but she didn't answer.

Instead, she tugged a tennis ball from her pocket and bounced it on the ground. "Want to play handball?"

I snapped my lunchbox shut. "Sure."

I hoped Ki would forget that she had asked me over to her place. I didn't want to meet the dangerous, **biting** Fangs at all.

Chapter 3

So, Are You Coming Over?

The bell rang. School was over for the day. I slipped out into the hall, hoping Ki wouldn't see me. I slid my stuff into my bag and turned around.

Ki was right behind me. Watching me. "Ready?" she asked.

"For what?" I said, pretending that I didn't know what she meant.

"To come to my place."

"Oh, I just remembered I have something on."

"Like what?" she asked.

"Ah, karate. Yeah, that's right."

Ki snorted. "No you don't. You do karate with me on Thursdays. Remember?"

My face went bright red. I was a terrible liar. "Oh, yeah. That's right."

"What's up?" Ki asked.

I rushed outside into the playground. "Nothing."

"So, are you coming over?"

"Mum might wonder where I am," I said.

"Well, she's over there with your sister." Ki pointed Mum out in the crowd. "Why don't you ask her now?"

"Good idea," I said, while inside I was groaning.

I trudged over to Mum. Ki walked happily beside me. I knew I was **stuck**. Unless Mum said no, I wouldn't get out of meeting Fangs. I was **doomed**!

Chapter 4

Come On, Max!

"Sure, you can go to Ki's," Mum said, just like I knew she would. Just like I hoped she wouldn't.

I nodded.

Silently, I was begging Mum to say no or to change her mind. She didn't do either. She took my sister's hand, and they walked away. I watched them leave, feeling like I was drowning.

"Come on," Ki said. "Let's go."

As we walked down the street to Ki's house, I came up with ways to slow us down.

I bounced my soccer ball along the footpath. Every few steps I dropped it, so I had to chase after it.

I looked at my shoe. I stopped to pick a stone out of my sock.

"Come on, Max!" Ki called back to me. "You're taking forever."

I tucked the soccer ball under my arm. I stopped to tie my shoelace. Another time, I stopped to look at a bird inside a tree.

"Are you all right?" Ki asked.

"Yeah. Why?"

"You're acting **weird**," she said.

"I'm fine," I said.

I couldn't tell her how I was really feeling. She would laugh at me or tease me. So I played it cool.

"By the way, how big is Fangs?"
I asked.

"**Huge,**" Ki said. "But he's going to grow a lot bigger. He never stops eating. You should see him."

"I can't wait," I said.

By now, I was imagining a huge monster with a lion's head and a dog's body. I imagined the monster snapping at my heels. Swallowing me whole.

Ki laughed. "Don't worry, you will love him."

I wasn't so sure. If only Ki would tell me what Fangs was, I might not have to worry. I was about to say so when Ki said, "Come on! Race you home!"

Ki took off. We often race each other and Ki often beats me. She's a fast runner and I hate losing to her, so I ran after her as fast as I could go.

Every step I took, I was closer to Fangs. And my **doom**. I was sure of it.

17

Chapter 5
Ki's Place

When we got to Ki's, I wiped my dry, clean shoes **slowly** and carefully on the front mat. I took as much time as I could get away with. I dreaded the thought of having to go inside and face Fangs.

We said hi to Ki's grandma, who was decorating a cake with cherry-coloured swirls in the kitchen.

"That looks yum," I said. "What sort of cake is it?"

"Cherry cheesecake," she said. "You can have some for afternoon tea. What are you two up to?"

"Max wants to see Fangs," Ki said.

"Well, not quite," I thought. "Actually, not at all."

"Oh." Ki's grandma gave me a worried look. "You'd better be careful," she said. "Fangs is really **scary**. Are you sure you can handle it?"

I gulped. "Sure. How bad can he be?"

I still had no idea what Fangs was or what he looked like. By now, I was thinking maybe he was a two-metre-long snake. Or maybe a crocodile.

Or, worse, maybe he was a dragon!

"Oh, he's pretty scary." Ki's grandma laughed. "He hasn't had dinner yet either, so he'll be hungry."

"H-h-hungry? H-h-how much does he normally eat?"

Ki's grandma's eyes twinkled. She grinned at me. "It's hard keeping him full some days. We have to go hunting for live food all over the house."

"Really?" I squeaked with fright. This pet not only ate meat, it ate **live** meat. Live animals. What kind of pet was it?

"Yep," Ki's grandma said.

"Come on," Ki said, dragging me inside. "He's in my room."

"You keep Fangs in your bedroom?"

"Best place for him."

21

Chapter 6
Meeting Fangs

Slowly, I followed Ki up the hall to her room. My feet were so heavy. It felt like I had bricks tied to them. Sweat ran down my face. My heart was doing frog-hops in my chest.

"Don't be afraid! Don't be afraid!" I chanted to myself.

We stopped outside Ki's door. I could feel my legs shaking.

Ki swung her door open. "Ta-dah!"

I peered inside the room. No monster jumped out to greet me. No dog barked. No cat hissed. Not even a mouse squeaked.

I took a cautious step inside.

"W-w-where is it?" I asked.

Ki pointed to the window.

"Outside?"

"On the window sill," Ki said.

Confused, I stepped closer. Something was on the window sill. It was a small, brown pot. And in the pot was a plant. A very strange looking plant.

"What is it?" I asked.

"That's Fangs."

"Fangs?"

"Yep. Fangs is a Venus flytrap."

"I can't believe I've been scared of a plant!" I thought.

The breath I was holding whooshed out of me. My heart slowed and stopped thumping. My forehead cooled down.

I'd been scared of a plant! But now I didn't need to be scared anymore.

"I thought you said Fangs was scary."

"He is." Ki laughed. "He's a death trap if you're a fly. So, do you want to feed him?"